Why do people have horses?

Written by Catherine Baker

Illustrated by Ángeles Peinador

Collins

What's in this book?

Listen and say

rider

horse

Download the audio at www.collins.co.uk/839695

horse-riding

5

I like horses and I like horse-riding.

I clean Lady, too. I clean her ears, her face, her legs, her back and her tail.

back

tail

legs

I give Lady and her baby food.
Horses eat grass and hay.

ear

face

Horse-riding is great. Some people ride their horses to the shops.

Horses can pull carts.

I am going to town.

cart

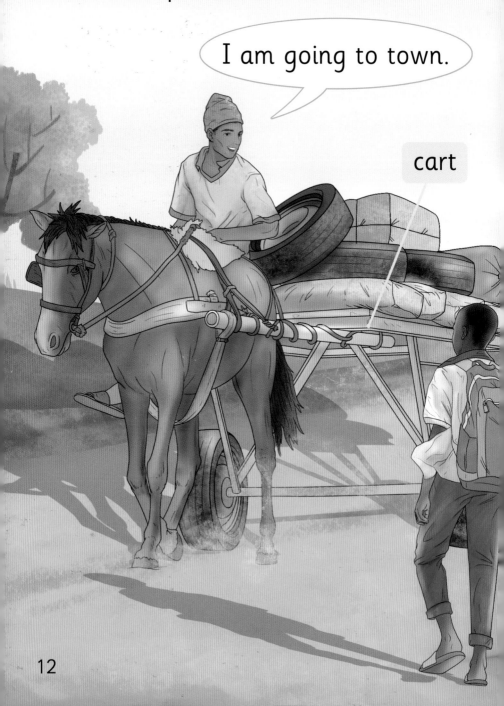

Horses are strong. They can pull
big carts. Look at the hay on this cart.

Look at the vegetables on this cart.

Horses can go on streets.

This horse is helping the police.

police

People have horses for sports.
These horses are running. It's a race.

This horse is jumping.

Mummy says, "I like horses. Do you like horses, Elsie?"

Elsie says, "Yes, I do. Can I go horse-riding please, Mummy?"

Mummy says, "Yes, Elsie. You can."

Picture dictionary

Listen and repeat

cart

grass

hay

horse

horse-riding

police

sport

vegetables

1 Look and match

run

pull

jump

2 Listen and say

Collins

Published by Collins
An imprint of HarperCollins*Publishers*
Westerhill Road
Bishopbriggs
Glasgow
G64 2QT

HarperCollins*Publishers*
1st Floor, Watermarque Building
Ringsend Road
Dublin 4
Ireland

William Collins' dream of knowledge for all began with the publication of his first book in 1819.

A self-educated mill worker, he not only enriched millions of lives, but also founded a flourishing publishing house. Today, staying true to this spirit, Collins books are packed with inspiration, innovation and practical expertise. They place you at the centre of a world of possibility and give you exactly what you need to explore it.

ISBN 978-0-00-839695-4

Collins® and COBUILD® are registered trademarks of HarperCollins*Publishers* Limited

www.collins.co.uk/elt

British Library Cataloguing in Publication Data

A catalogue record for this publication is available from the British Library.

Author: Catherine Baker
Illustrator: Ángeles Peinador (Beehive)
Series editor: Rebecca Adlard
Commissioning editor: Zoë Clarke
Publishing manager: Lisa Todd
Product managers: Jennifer Hall and Caroline Green
In-house editor: Alma Puts Keren
Project manager: Emily Hooton
Editor: Tessie Papadopoulou-Dalton
Proofreaders: Natalie Murray and Michael Lamb
Cover designer: Kevin Robbins
Typesetter: 2Hoots Publishing Services Ltd
Audio produced by id audio, London
Reading guide author: Emma Wilkinson
Production controller: Rachel Weaver
Printed and bound by: GPS Group, Slovenia

MIX
Paper from
responsible sources
FSC™ C007454

This book is produced from independently certified FSC™ paper to ensure responsible forest management.

For more information visit: **www.harpercollins.co.uk/green**

Download the audio for this book and a reading guide for parents and teachers at www.collins.co.uk/839695